Teachers, librarians, and kids from across Canada are talking about the *Canadian Flyer Adventures.* Here's what some of them had to say:

Great Canadian historical content, excellent illustrations, and superb closing historical facts (I love the kids' commentary!). ~ *SARA S., TEACHER, ONTARIO*

As a teacher–librarian I welcome this series with open arms. It fills the gap for Canadian historical adventures at an early reading level! There's fast action, interesting, believable characters, and great historical information. ~ *MARGARET L., TEACHER–LIBRARIAN, BRITISH COLUMBIA*

The *Canadian Flyer Adventures* will transport young readers to different eras of our past with their appealing topics. Thank goodness there are more artifacts in that old dresser ... they are sure to lead to even more escapades. ~ *SALLY B., TEACHER–LIBRARIAN, MANITOBA*

When I shared the book with a grade 1–2 teacher at my school, she enjoyed the book, noting that her students would find it appealing because of the action-adventure and short chapters. ~ *HEATHER J., TEACHER AND LIBRARIAN, NOVA SCOTIA*

Newly independent readers will fly through each *Canadian Flyer Adventure*, and be asking for the next installment! Children will enjoy the fast-paced narrative, the personalities of the main characters, and the drama of the dangerous situations the children find themselves in. ~ *PAM L., LIBRARIAN, ONTARIO*

I love the fact that these are Canadian adventures—kids should know how exciting Canadian history is. Emily and Matt are regular kids, full of curiosity, and I can see readers relating to them. ~ JEAN K., TEACHER, ONTARIO

What kids told us:

I would like to have the chance to ride on a magical sled and have adventures. ~ EMMANUEL

I would like to tell the author that her book is amazing, incredible, awesome, and a million times better than any book I've read. ~ MARIA

I would recommend the *Canadian Flyer Adventures* series to other kids so they could learn about Canada too. The book is just the right length and hard to put down. ~ PAUL

The books I usually read are the full-of-fact encyclopedias. This book is full of interesting ideas that simply grab me. ~ ELEANOR

At the end of the book Matt and Emily say they are going on another adventure. I'm very interested in where they are going next! ~ ALEX

I like when Emily and Matt fly into the sky on a sled towards a new adventure. I can't wait for the next book! ~ JI SANG

Stop that Stagecoach!

Frieda Wishinsky

Illustrated by Jean-Paul Eid

MAPLE
TREE
PRESS

For my friend, Ettie Shuken

Many thanks to the hard-working Maple Tree/Owlkids team, for their insightful comments and steadfast support. Special thanks to Jean-Paul Eid and Barb Kelly for their engaging and energetic illustrations and design.

Maple Tree Press books are published by Owlkids Books Inc.
10 Lower Spadina Avenue, Suite 400, Toronto, Ontario M5V 2Z2
www.owlkids.com

Text © 2009 Frieda Wishinsky   Illustrations © 2009 Jean-Paul Eid

Distributed in Canada by Raincoast Books
9050 Shaughnessy Street, Vancouver, British Columbia V6P 6E5

Distributed in the United States by Publishers Group West
1700 Fourth Street, Berkeley, California 94710

Library and Archives Canada Cataloguing in Publication

Wishinsky, Frieda
Stop that stagecoach! / Frieda Wishinsky ; illustrated by Jean-Paul Eid.

(Canadian flyer adventures ; 13)
ISBN 978-1-897349-62-5 (bound).--ISBN 978-1-897349-63-2 (pbk.)

1. Frontier and pioneer life--Ontario--Juvenile fiction. I. Eid, Jean-Paul
II. Title. III. Series: Wishinsky, Frieda. Canadian flyer adventures ; 13.

PS8595.I834S86 2009   jC813'.54   C2009-903886-2

Library of Congress Control Number: 2009930916

Canada Council   Conseil des Arts
for the Arts   du Canada

ONTARIO ARTS COUNCIL
CONSEIL DES ARTS DE L'ONTARIO

We acknowledge the financial support of the Canada Council for the Arts, the Ontario Arts Council, the Government of Canada through the Book Publishing Industry Development Program (BPIDP), and the Government of Ontario through the Ontario Media Development Corporation's Book Initiative for our publishing activities.

Printed in Canada
Ancient Forest Friendly: Printed on 100% Post-Consumer Recycled Paper

Manufactured by Friesens Corporation
Manufactured in Altona, MB, Canada in September, 2009
Job# 49292

A   B   C   D   E   F

CONTENTS

HOW IT ALL BEGAN

Emily and Matt couldn't believe their luck. They discovered an old dresser full of strange objects in the tower of Emily's house. They also found a note from Emily's Great-Aunt Miranda: "The sled is yours. Fly it to wonderful adventures."

They found a sled right behind the dresser! When they sat on it, shimmery gold words appeared:

Rub the leaf
Three times fast.
Soon you'll fly
To the past.

The sled rose over Emily's house. It flew over their town of Glenwood. It sailed out of a cloud and into the past. Their adventures on the flying sled had begun! Where will the sled take them next? Turn the page to find out.

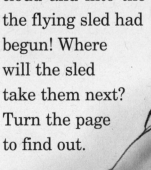

Baby Blanket,
Upper Canada,
June 1833

1

Back Then

Emily stared at her pencil. She'd rubbed out her words so many times, there was nothing left of the eraser.

"Hey, Em. What are you doing?" asked Matt. He bounded up the porch stairs.

"I'm writing a story for school. It's about what it was like to travel to Canada in the early 1800s. Then we're supposed to read our stories in front of the whole school."

"Awesome!" said Matt. He sat beside Emily on the white wicker couch.

Emily groaned. "It's not awesome. It's awful! I can't do this story."

"Why not?" Matt pointed to a pile of books. "Don't those help?"

"A little, but they're full of dates and places. I can't tell what it was really like back then."

Matt winked. "You need to go there," he said.

Emily's eyes lit up. "You're right! Then I'd know exactly what to write. Come on. Let's see what's in the tower. I bet there's something in the dresser that will fly us to the 1800s on the magic sled."

Matt grinned. "Good old sled. It always knows where to take us."

Emily opened the front door. "Do you have your digital recorder with you?"

"Of course! I'm always ready to record anything exciting that happens.

And something always does."

Emily patted the pocket of her jeans. "And I'm always ready to draw. After all our trips on the sled, my sketchbook is almost full."

They raced up the rickety stairs to the tower room. Emily pushed the door open and headed for the old mahogany dresser.

"Let's check out the top drawer," said Matt.

Emily pulled it open. As soon as she did, she saw a faded piece of white knitted cloth labelled Baby Blanket, Upper Canada, June 1833.

"Perfect!" she exclaimed. "Looks like we're going to see a baby somewhere in Ontario. My teacher told us that Ontario used to be called Upper Canada."

Matt picked up the sled from behind the dresser. "I like babies," he said, "as long as they don't spit up on me."

Emily laughed. "I like them as long as they don't cry all the time."

Emily and Matt hopped on the sled. The magic words immediately appeared.

Rub the leaf
Three times fast.
Soon you'll fly
To the past.

Emily rubbed the leaf, and the sled was enveloped in fog. Then it rose over her house, over Glenwood, and straight into a fluffy white cloud.

2

Goofy Hats

"I see a ship!" Matt called as the sled burst out of the cloud.

"Look at those big white sails blowing in the wind," said Emily.

The sled dipped lower and lower. It veered away from the ship and bumped down on a cobblestone road near the harbour.

Matt and Emily slid off.

Emily looked down at her clothes. The magic always gave them just the right clothes for the adventure.

"How do you like this long blue cotton dress?" she asked, twirling around.

"It's fine except for the goofy bonnet. What do you think of my outfit?"

"You look good in those short pants, and I like your little black cap. We're both wearing goofy hats on this adventure. And we each have a bag with extra clothes." Emily pointed to the ground. Two stuffed canvas bags leaned against the sled.

"I bet this will be a long adventure," said Matt. "I even have a bag of coins." Matt pulled out a small canvas bag from his pocket.

Emily checked her pockets. "I have coins, too. We're in the money!"

"Good old magic! But exactly where are we?"

"Let's ask that boy over there," suggested Emily.

A sandy-haired boy of about eleven was

lugging a heavy bag over his shoulders and dragging a battered trunk across the ground.

Matt ran over and patted him on the back. The boy turned around.

"Excuse me," said Matt. "But what's the name of this place?"

"Don't you know?" asked the boy.

"We're a little lost," said Emily, dashing over to join them.

"This is Montreal," said the boy.

"Montreal!" said Emily. "Wow! We are really lost. We want to go to Upper Canada."

The boy smiled. "That is where my mother and I are going, too. My father is building a home for us there. Are you travelling with your family?"

"We're meeting up with them...later," said Matt.

The boy put down his bags and extended

his hand. "My name is Thomas O'Brien."

"I'm Matt, and this is Emily."

"Perhaps you would like to travel with us?" suggested Thomas.

"We would!" said Emily.

"Let me speak to my mother. She is sitting over there on that crate. She is going to have a baby soon, and she tires easily."

Thomas hurried over to his mother. Soon he was back. "Mother said she would be delighted to have you join us. Come over and meet her."

3

Bumpy Road

Clang! Clang! Clang!

The sound of bells rang through the air.

Thomas stopped walking and looked up at the houses nearby. Fear spread across his face.

"What's the matter?" asked Emily.

"Those bells mean there has been another death in Montreal. There have been so many deaths here already."

Emily shivered. "Why are so many people dying?"

"It is the cholera disease. We thought we were safe on board, but a man from our ship took ill. We have been lucky so far, but now we must leave Montreal. We do not want to come down with this terrible sickness, too."

"I'm ready to get out of here right now," said Matt.

"Let me ask Mother when the stagecoach is due to arrive. It will take us on the first part of our journey," said Thomas. He ran ahead.

Emily clapped her hands. "I've always wanted to ride in a stagecoach. I hope there are no masked bandits on the road who will demand all our money and jewels, like they do in the movies!"

Matt laughed. "That only happened out west in cowboy country."

Thomas waved to them. He introduced them to his mother.

Mrs. O'Brien told them that the stagecoach would arrive soon. "I want to leave this place quickly," she said, peering up at the stone buildings and churches dotting Montreal. "There is nothing here but disease. I long to join Mr. O'Brien in our new homestead near Peterborough. Will you children be going all the way with us?"

"Some of the way, for sure," said Emily.

Emily and Matt could tell that Mrs. O'Brien was about to ask them more questions, but the stagecoach arrived just in time.

"Hurry!" shouted the stagecoach driver, hustling them inside. "I do not want to stay in this plague-ridden city for another moment."

Emily and Matt looked up at the unshaven, burly coachman. They stared at the two bony horses that pulled the large rickety stagecoach. It was hard to believe those two

scrawny creatures would be able to pull such a big coach.

Mrs. O'Brien stood up slowly and gathered her bags. The stagecoach driver used heavy rope to tie the trunk and bags to the railing on top of the coach. He reached for the sled, but Matt stopped him.

"We want to keep that inside with us."

"I hope our belongings will not fall off," said Thomas eying the pile on top of the coach. Then he helped his mother inside.

Thomas sat beside his mother on the rough, tattered stagecoach seats. Matt and Emily sat across from them. Matt shoved the sled under their seat.

"Giddy-up!" shouted the coachman, and they were off.

The coach rattled down the bumpy Montreal streets. It passed a towering cathedral, soldiers' barracks, stone buildings, and houses. Many doors were draped in black. "That means someone died inside that house," Thomas explained.

They drove on past open sewers and streets strewn with garbage. The air smelled so awful it made them gasp and cough.

"Soon we will be in the country," said Mrs. O'Brien, covering her mouth with an embroidered white handkerchief. "It will be better there."

"It will smell better, for sure," said Matt.

"It will, unless we pass farms with pigs and cows," said Emily. "But I bet one day Montreal will smell much better than this."

Matt grinned. "I bet it will, too."

4

All Shook Up

The stagecoach drove toward the open countryside. Soon the air smelled cleaner, and they could see grassy fields, tall trees, and pink and white spring flowers.

"Now this is more like it!" said Matt.

"It is so good to see trees and flowers, but I wish this carriage did not rattle so much," said Mrs. O'Brien. "The roads back home in Ireland were smoother. You cannot even call these roads. They are just holes and broken wood planks."

"I know," said Emily. "Every time we hit a rut, I feel like a milkshake."

"Milkshake?" asked Thomas. "What is that? Why would anyone shake milk?"

Emily glanced at Matt. Oh no! How could she explain to Thomas and his mother what a milkshake was? Emily didn't even know if they could get ice cream in the early 1830s.

"A milkshake is a special drink made of milk and sweet syrup," she said, carefully choosing each word. "You mix it up by shaking it. We have it at home, and it's foamy and delicious."

"We must try a milkshake when we are settled in our new home," said Mrs. O'Brien. "Right now the thought of food makes my stomach heave."

Matt and Emily glanced at Mrs. O'Brien. She looked like she was about to be sick.

"Do you want us to ask the coachman to stop?" Emily asked.

Mrs. O'Brien took a deep breath. "No, I think I can make it a little while longer."

"Look. There's an inn! We will be stopping soon, and we can get out of this terrible coach," said Thomas.

"Thank goodness," murmured Mrs. O' Brien.

The inn was a three-storey stone building with a half-rotted wooden sign dangling from the front porch. It read: Mrs. Crowley's Inn.

The coach stopped.

Thomas and Matt helped Mrs. O'Brien out.

"It's going to be such fun staying at an old-fashioned inn!" Emily whispered to Matt. "I bet they bake fresh cookies and serve bread with churned butter and homemade marmalade. Mmm."

But before they reached the front door, it swung open. A bearded man in ragged clothes raced out, followed by a heavy frying pan flying through the air. The pan looked like it was going to hit the man, but it missed and clanged on the ground. The man dashed

to the back of the inn. Soon he returned riding on a horse so thin you could see its ribs.

A minute later, a short, plump woman waddled out of the inn. She shook her fist at the man and shouted, "You are lucky this time, you no-good freeloader! Do not come back to my inn again, or next time my frying pan will hit its mark. No one stays at Mrs. Crowley's without paying for the pleasure!"

5

Squished

"I'm not sure this inn is going to be as much fun as I thought," Emily whispered to Matt as Mrs. Crowley cursed the man riding off on his scrawny horse.

"He won't get far on that miserable beast," Mrs. Crowley sneered. Then she turned to Mrs. O'Brien. "So, what can I do for you?"

"We would like a room for the night," said Mrs. O'Brien.

"As of today, my customers will have to pay in advance," said Mrs. Crowley. "And you will all have to share a bed, except for you, ma'am. I make exceptions for women in your condition."

"Thank you," said Mrs. O'Brien. "We will pay in advance."

"We have money to pay, too," said Emily.

"Good. That comes with supper and breakfast. Follow me," said Mrs. Crowley.

The group followed Mrs. Crowley into the main room of the inn. A few candles dimly lit the space. A long, rough wooden table covered with chipped platters and dirty bowls stood in the centre of the room. Chunks of stale bread littered the floor. Gobs of porridge stuck to the edges of the table. Flies buzzed around and settled on the leftovers.

"This way," said Mrs. Crowley. They followed her up a set of crooked stairs to a small room crammed with two large beds and one small one. Each bed had a sagging feather mattress, and the room smelled like no one had opened a window for days. The linens on the beds were a greyish white.

"This room is where the ladies will sleep," said Mrs. Crowley, yanking open the room's one small window. "Now, that's much better."

Emily winced. The room still smelled stale. And who else was going to sleep here besides Mrs. O'Brien?

"Mrs. Smith and her four grown daughters will share the two beds with you, young lady," said Mrs. Crowley, turning to Emily. "They are large women, and it will be a bit tight. The small bed is yours, Mrs. O'Brien. Now, you boys follow me to the men's sleeping quarters. It will be tight there, too. The coachman has requested a bed, and you will share with him."

Matt and Thomas gave each other a look of despair. Matt knew that Thomas didn't want to sleep beside the bellowing, unwashed coachman either.

But what could they do?

"Now, you may join me in the dining room for supper." Mrs. Crowley's voice was softer now. "There's leftover potato soup and brown bread."

"Is that all there is for supper?" groaned Emily. "I thought this inn was going to be nice. It is not nice at all!"

6

Muddy Soup

"I am not sleeping in that bed with two women," said Emily. "I'll only have a speck of space in bed. I'd rather sleep outside."

"I'd rather sleep outside, too, than share a bed with that coachman," said Matt, rolling his eyes.

"There is no mattress outside, and it may get chilly late at night," said Mrs. O'Brien.

"It can't be worse than being squished like a tomato. I'll put on all my clothes to stay warm," said Emily.

"Me too," said Matt.

"I will try to sleep in the bed," said Thomas. "I am so tired I will fall asleep even if the coachman snores."

"And stinks?" asked Emily.

"Even stink will not bother me tonight," said Thomas, yawning.

Mrs. O'Brien shook her head. "Children, please reconsider sleeping outside. Ah, here comes Mrs. Crowley with our supper."

Mrs. Crowley placed a bowl of hot soup

in front of each of them. A few bits of potato and one thin slice of onion floated in each bowl of brownish liquid. She plunked a loaf of brown bread on the table.

"There is no butter today, but the bread is only two days old. All you need is to chew it well, and it will soften up. You are lucky, for I have just made this batch of strawberry preserves. Now I must attend to my rabbits and chickens."

Then Mrs. Crowley waddled out of the dining room toward the front door.

Matt took a spoonful of soup. "This tastes like...like..."

"Soapy water?" said Emily.

"Yes," said Matt. "The soup is disgusting."

"And the bread is as hard as stone, but the strawberry preserves are scrumptious," said Emily.

Mrs. O'Brien picked away at the potato and spooned some preserves on a small piece of bread. "I long to bake my own bread and make my own soup. It will be good to be settled in my own home."

"Mother is the best cook in the world. Everyone back home loved dining with our family," said Thomas. "I will close my eyes and imagine that this terrible soup is one of yours, Mother. That will surely help it taste better."

Thomas closed his eyes and sipped some potato soup.

"Does imagining help it taste better?" asked Emily.

Thomas shook his head and laughed. "No. It still tastes like mud, but the preserves are wonderful." Thomas slathered a piece of bread with the preserves. All three children licked the preserves off the bread.

"Children," Mrs. O'Brien chided them. "That is not the proper way to eat bread."

"But, Mother," said Thomas. "This is not proper bread. If I don't eat some preserves, I will starve."

Mrs. O'Brien smiled. "You are right, Thomas. This is the worst meal I have ever had. It is even less edible than the miserable food on the ship. Now, what have you two decided about tonight?"

"I still want to sleep outside, Mrs. O'Brien," said Matt. "I'm going to get my things and head out. It's not too cold out."

"There might be some wild animals around," said Thomas.

"There couldn't be anything really scary here," said Matt. "There might be some squirrels, deer, or rabbits. There aren't any lions or tigers."

"But there might be some bears," said Thomas.

"Well, we don't have any food for them, so bears will leave us alone," said Emily.

"Absolutely," said Matt, but when Emily looked at his face, she saw Matt was worried that there might be some unfriendly animal lurking in the woods.

7

Only Me

Emily sat down on the ground and pulled out her sketchbook. "Before it gets dark, I want to draw a picture of us camping outside."

Matt slid his recorder out of his pocket and flipped it on. "Emily and I are sleeping outside somewhere in Upper Canada. It's cool outside, but we're wearing extra clothes, and we have two blankets each so we should be warm."

Emily put the finishing touches on her drawing and pulled two blankets over her shoulders. "I'm ready to go to sleep," she said, yawning.

"I'm tired, too," said Matt. He snapped off his recorder.

Emily closed her eyes. She was almost asleep when she heard footsteps. They were coming closer and closer.

She poked Matt in the back. "Someone's here," she whispered.

"It is only me," said a voice.

Matt and Emily looked up. Thomas was standing beside them. He was carrying two

blankets and wearing layers of clothing.

"I could not sleep. The coachman snored so loudly the bed shook," said Thomas.

"Well, there's lots of room here," said Matt.

Thomas placed the blankets on the ground and lay down. "Have you seen any wild animals?" he asked.

"Not even one," said Emily, closing her eyes again.

"Oh, that is good," murmured Thomas and he closed his eyes, too.

Emily woke up first. Something was licking her face.

"Cut that out," she shouted, opening her eyes. It was morning. The sun was blinding, and for a minute she couldn't see what was licking her face. Then she blinked and saw it was a little brown dog.

"Well, where did you come from?" asked Matt.

"Look over there!" said Emily.

Mrs. Crowley was standing at the door of the inn. "Breakfast, Rupert!" she called. The little dog bounded up to her and licked her hand. She patted him gently on the head. It was clear Mrs. Crowley liked her dog more than she liked the people who stayed at her inn.

"Come in for porridge, you three," Mrs. Crowley called. "If you do not hurry, there will be none left."

Mrs. Crowley and Rupert headed inside.

Emily, Matt, and Thomas looked at each other. "If her porridge tastes anything like her soup, I do not want to eat even a mouthful," said Thomas.

"Yeah. Who cares if there's none left?" said Emily.

"I'm really hungry," said Matt. "Maybe it will be good."

Emily made a face. "I doubt it, but we might as well check it out. I'm hungry, too."

The three friends trooped inside. Thomas's mother was sitting at the table alone. She smiled when she saw them.

"Did you sleep well?" she asked Emily and Matt.

"Pretty well," said Matt. "There were only a few interruptions."

Thomas laughed. "I joined them outside, Mother," he explained. "The coachman's snores were so loud that I could not sleep. How do you feel?"

Mrs. O'Brien sighed. "I am tired. The women in my room snored so loudly that it was like some horrible music. One started and then stopped. Then another started and stopped.

But there is one good thing to report. The porridge is tasty."

"Great!" said Emily, and she dipped her spoon into the bowl. "Mmm. You're right."

The coachman strode into the room as everyone finished breakfast.

"We leave in ten minutes," he barked.

Thomas and Mrs. O'Brien rushed to gather up their belongings. Emily and Matt waited for them on the front porch.

"I wonder how long this trip is going to be?" said Matt.

"Wouldn't it be great if the sled could just fly us there?" said Emily. "Then we wouldn't have to sit in that bumpy coach again."

Matt laughed. "I thought you wanted to ride in a stagecoach."

"Not anymore," said Emily.

8

Slide

For the next week, they rattled along the Upper Canada roads and stopped at more inns.

In one, they ate fresh bread and butter, but in most the food was awful, the beds uncomfortable, and their sleeping companions noisy. Emily, Matt, and Thomas spent many nights sleeping under the stars.

To pass the time and distract them from the uncomfortable ride, Emily and Matt taught Thomas and his mother how to play I Spy with My Little Eye. Everyone had fun guessing what the person who was "it" saw and was thinking about.

One day, Emily saw a skunk, three rabbits, two squirrels, five farmers, and a deer. Matt saw two log cabins, three black horses, and a scarecrow. Thomas saw two boys working in the fields and a cap dangling from a tree. Mrs. O'Brien saw a small broken wooden box left on a stump.

On the eighth day, they headed for the steamer that would take them across Lake Ontario. They were nearing the dock where the steamer was tied up when the coach began to shake and tilt.

"Hurry! Slide to the left!" shouted the coachman.

Everyone slid to the left as the coach swayed. Emily grabbed Matt's arm. Matt swallowed hard. Mrs. O'Brien turned white, and Thomas held his mother's hand as the coach lurched back and forth like a see-saw. It felt like they were going to tip over!

And then the stagecoach jerked to a stop. "Everyone out," called the coachman. "This is as far as I go."

The coachmen began to toss everyone's bags off the top of the coach.

"Please be careful," said Mrs. O'Brien. "I have some delicate items tucked in between my clothes."

"I am not responsible if anything breaks," snapped the coachman. "My job was to get you here, and I have. I am off now." He sat back up on the wagon and tapped his horse with a whip. "Giddy-up."

Luckily, the steamer was only a short walk away. Matt and Emily helped Mrs. O'Brien and Thomas carry their belongings. They put

some on the sled, and Matt pulled the sled till they reached the dock.

When they found seats on the boat, Mrs. O'Brien opened one of her bags. "I hope my mother's teacups have survived the journey," she said as she unfolded a shawl. "I should have kept them inside the coach, but I never dreamed the coachman would handle everything so roughly."

Inside the shawl lay two delicate blue and white teacups. "Thank goodness they are not broken. I have four of these teacups, and they are precious to me."

Then she pulled out a long nightgown and unfolded it. One teacup was intact. The other one had broken into hundreds of pieces.

Tears rolled down Mrs. O'Brien cheeks. "These teacups remind me of my family and home."

Thomas put his arm around his mother's shoulders.

Mrs. O'Brien wiped her eyes. "Thank you, Thomas, but I will be fine. They are just bits of china. The important thing is that I have you, the new baby is coming, and soon we will be reunited with your father."

"It is good to leave that awful coach behind," said Thomas.

"You're not kidding," said Emily. "I was sure we were all going to get broken like that teacup."

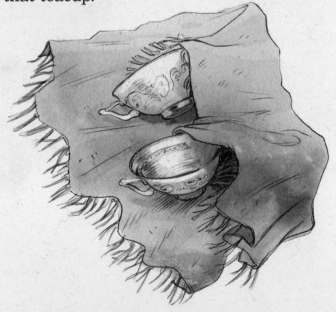

9

Where Can We Go?

Mrs. O'Brien patted Emily's hand. "Yes. Thank goodness, we are all in one piece, and the air smells sweet here. Lake Ontario is so calm and beautiful today. There is much to like about this new land."

A few hours later, they reached the settlement of Cobourg. Thomas pointed to a wagon. "We take that next," he said.

"I hope it's more comfortable than the coach," said Emily.

"I hope it doesn't spill us on the ground.

I can still feel that coach shaking us like a milkshake," said Matt, winking at Emily.

The light wagon, as this carriage was called, was pulled by four sturdy horses. The driver was friendlier than the coachman. Best of all, the wagon was lined with buffalo rugs, so they didn't feel as rattled by each bump in the road.

Two days after they stepped into the light wagon, they took another steamer across Rice Lake and up the Otonabee River.

Peterborough

Otonabee River

Rice Lake

Cobourg

Lake Ontario

This steamer ride was pleasant, too. They could see farms and homes dotting the countryside.

Then they transferred to a scow, a large, flat-bottomed rowboat. They were joined by two other travellers, Samuel Brand and his twelve-year-old son, Richard. The scow was the only boat that could navigate the shallow waters of the river.

But as soon as the boat left the shore, they knew they were in trouble. The oarsmen

were drunk. They bellowed. They cursed. They sang loud sea shanties as they loaded everyone's belongings up high.

"I hope these men do not tip us or our belongings into the river," said Mr. Brand.

Emily nodded. They were all worried about the same thing.

And then the scow reached the rapids.

"We are not taking this boat down these rapids tonight," said one of the oarsmen.

"We will wait here till tomorrow," said another.

"We cannot stay in this open boat all night. It is cold and wet. There is no place to lie down," said Mrs. O'Brien.

"That is not our problem," said one of the rowers. "I can sleep standing up. So can my friends."

"I can't sleep standing up," said Emily, but

the oarsmen just laughed.

"We cannot stay here. I am chilled to the bone," said Thomas.

"But where can we go?" asked Matt.

"Do not worry. Richard and I will lead you out," said Mr. Brand. "We had not planned to walk, but it is better than staying on this wretched boat or sleeping in the open on the riverbank."

Everyone looked at the oarsmen, who were sprawled across the deck of the scow they'd anchored to the shore. They were sound asleep and snoring.

"Richard and I know these woods well. The moon is bright and the night is lit up with stars. We will help you carry your bags and your trunk," Mr. Brand assured them.

"Thank you. That is kind of you," said Mrs. O'Brien.

"But, Mother. How can you walk, even a little?" asked Thomas.

"We have no choice," said Mrs. O'Brien. "We cannot stay here."

"B...but the baby...," said Thomas.

Mrs. O'Brien looked down at her bulging stomach. "This baby will have to wait till we reach a safe place. Let us go."

10

Follow Us

Everyone picked up as many bags as they could carry and stepped off the scow. They left the other belongings under a tree. Mr. Brand promised to come back and retrieve them in a few days.

Emily and Matt piled a few bags on their sled, and Matt dragged it behind him. Mr. Brand held up a lantern and everyone followed him down a trail. The stars and moon helped them see their way, but they still stumbled over logs and sank into mud.

"I am so tired," said Matt.

"Me, too," said Emily. "I feel like I'm lifting bricks instead of my legs."

"We must keep going," said Mr. Brand.

Emily sighed. "I know. If Mrs. O'Brien can keep going, then so can I. But sometimes it feels good to complain."

Everyone laughed.

"I am afraid I can no longer keep going. I must stop now," said Mrs. O'Brien suddenly. "I think...I think...the baby is coming!"

"We may be close to a house or an inn," said Mr. Brand. "Can you walk just a little farther?"

"I...I...don't know," said Mrs. O'Brien. "The pain is severe."

"We have to do something," said Thomas. He looked at his mother's face. She was biting her lips and breathing heavily.

"I'll run ahead with Richard. Maybe we can find some help," suggested Matt.

"Hurry!" said Mr. Brand. "We will wait here."

Matt and Richard raced along the trail. The other four travellers sat on a log.

Emily sat beside Mrs. O'Brien and held her hand. "You can squeeze my hand as hard as you want," said Emily.

Mrs. O'Brien smiled weakly. "Thank you, Emily. I just pray there is a house close by."

No one said anything more as they waited. But Emily knew they were all thinking the same thing. What if the baby came before they reached a house?

And then a faint voice rang through the night.

"We found a farmhouse! It's close!"

Mrs. O'Brien groaned and squeezed Emily's

hand. "We have to hurry!" said Emily.

To everyone's joy, the two boys approached. Mr. Brand and Thomas helped Mrs. O'Brien walk. She moaned with each step and stopped often to take a breath. They were all sure she'd have the baby right there on the trail. They knew it wasn't far to reach the house, but the trail seemed to go on and on.

And then they saw a small farmhouse!

A short, skinny woman met them at the door.

"Come in. We will help you," said the woman. "My name is Mrs. Cook. I have had six children of my own, and you will be fine."

Mrs. O'Brien nodded weakly.

Emily and Matt left the sled behind the farmhouse and joined everyone inside.

Mrs. Cook led Mrs. O'Brien into a bedroom. "The rest of you wait here," she said.

11

A New Baby

Thomas paced back and forth as they waited. Mr. Cook and two of his children offered the tired travellers hot potato soup.

"Potato soup?" Emily whispered to Matt.

Matt nodded. He knew what Emily meant. The last time they had potato soup it tasted awful.

Emily sipped a little of the soup. "This soup is delicious," she said. "Mrs. Cook is a terrific cook."

"It is wonderful soup," said Thomas.

"Thank you for all your help."

"We are glad to help a new neighbour," said Mr. Cook. "We heard that you and your mother were coming. Your father should be here in a few days. He left you this letter."

Mr. Cook reached into his pocket and pulled out a folded piece of paper. "In all the excitement, I almost forgot about it."

Thomas read the letter quickly. "Father says our homestead is almost built! He says we have good neighbours who will help us. He returns soon from Peterborough, where he is purchasing glass for windows."

"That's great," said Matt. "Listen! Did you hear that?"

It was a baby crying!

Mrs. Cook opened the bedroom door. She was beaming. "Your mother is fine, Thomas. Come meet your new baby sister."

Thomas rushed inside. Soon he was back in the main room. His eyes were shining. "Mother wants to see everyone. She wants you to meet my new baby sister. She is beautiful."

Everyone trooped into the small bedroom.

The baby lay beside a pale but smiling Mrs. O'Brien. The baby was wrapped in a small white blanket. It looked like the scrap of blanket Emily and Matt had found in the dresser!

"Thank you all for your kindness," said Mrs. O'Brien. "I could not have managed without you and neither could my little girl, Emma Sarah O'Brien. Can you guess why I named her that?"

"Is the Em part of her name for me?" asked Emily. "And the ma part for Matt?"

Mrs. O'Brien nodded.

"And is the Sa part of her middle name for

Samuel Brand, and the rah part for Richard?" asked Matt.

"That is exactly what I have done," said Mrs. O'Brien. "We will always remember how you helped bring us safely to this farmhouse."

"Wow!" said Emily. "No one has ever named a baby after me. Well, quarter-named a baby after me."

"Even a quarter-name is awesome!" said Matt, beaming.

"It is a great honour," said Mr. Brand.

"Now, leave Mrs. O'Brien to rest. Giving birth is a tiring business," said Mrs. Cook. She shooed them out of the bedroom.

When they returned to the main room, Matt peeked out the small window. "It's starting to rain. We'd better check on our sled, Em. We don't want it to get soaked."

Emily and Matt raced outside.

They hurried to the back of the farmhouse.

"Look!" said Emily. "Words are forming on the sled."

The trail was rough.
You made it though.
Now sit right down.
It's time to go.

"We have to fly home," said Emily.

"But we can't leave just like that. We have to tell everyone in the farmhouse. They'll worry about us."

"I know," said Emily. She opened her sketchbook and drew a picture of a baby. Under it she wrote:

Welcome, Emma Sarah!
And thank you all, but
we have to move on now.
Don't worry. We'll be fine.
*   - Emily and Matt.*

Then she ripped the page out, ran to the front of the farmhouse, and slipped the paper under the front door.

She dashed back to Matt. "Now let's go."

The friends hopped onto the sled. Immediately it rose over the farmhouse, over the Upper Canada trails, and into a fluffy white cloud.

Soon they were back in Emily's tower room. They slid off the sled.

"The sled is much smoother to ride than a stagecoach," said Matt.

Emily laughed. "The sled is the best! And now I'm ready to write that story for school. It will be full of amazing facts. Only no one will know how I learned them!" said Emily.

"Sometimes I wish we could tell someone

about the magic, but they'd never believe us." Matt pointed to the clock "It's awesome. No matter how long we are away on an adventure, time always stands still while we're gone."

"I know, and you know what else? I'm still hungry from this adventure. I only had a little of that yummy potato soup Mrs. Cook made before Emma Sarah was born. Let's see what's in the fridge. What would you like to eat?"

"Do you have any milk and cookies?" asked Matt.

"I'm sure we have some. Mom made potato cookies yesterday from an old family recipe."

"I've never heard of potato cookies. Are you kidding?"

Emily opened her eyes wide. "Me? Kid you? Puh-lease!" Then she winked. "Of course I'm kidding. We have double fudge cookies—with mashed potato icing!"

MORE ABOUT...

After their adventure, Matt and Emily wanted to know more about life in pioneer times. Turn the page for their favourite facts.

Emily's Top Ten Facts

1. Over 30,000 immigrants a year came to Quebec in the 1830s. About two-thirds of them were from Ireland.

2. Because many people were sick with cholera in Britain, immigrants had to stop at Grosse Isle, Quebec, where they were inspected for the disease. If they were sick, they were sent to special sheds on the island to keep them away from healthy people.

3. In the 1830s, entire families died from cholera in Montreal.

4. Doctors in Upper Canada were sometimes paid with animals instead of money. One doctor said he received five ducks for helping a patient.

5. Many people in the mid-1800s only took hot baths as a medical treatment.

6. In the 1830s, people often lost all their teeth by the time they were thirty-five.

7. Beds were full of fleas, and lice were everywhere.

Am I glad we didn't sleep in those inns! Imagine all those fleas and lice!

—M.

8. People in the 1830s would dress baby girls in many layers: skirts, petticoats, and a top, with a robe or dress over everything else.

9. Making candles was important in the 1830s because candles were used to light rooms. Electricity wasn't invented till the late 1800s.

10. People first used the word "milkshake" in 1885, but those milkshakes used whisky and eggs. Milkshakes with ice cream weren't made till around 1900.

No Ice cream? Yuck!

—M.

Matt's Top Ten Facts

1. Here are some chores boys did in the 1830s: gathered wood for fires, rounded up cattle, helped in the fields, and carried water.

2. Here are some chores that girls did: spun, wove, cleaned candlesticks, knitted, and helped take care of younger brothers and sisters.

> How come the boys didn't help take care of the younger kids, too? —E.

3. Pine was the most popular wood used by colonial craftspeople.

4. If you owned a good wooden clock, people were impressed.

5. Cherries, apples, pears, peaches, and grapes were grown in many parts of Canada in the early 1800s.

6. Settlers loved to have parties called "bees" to help their neighbours or to celebrate an event. There were barn-raising bees, corn-husking bees, and quilting bees.

7. There was a lot of dancing at the bees. Some popular dances were mazurkas, reels, and jigs.

8. Lamb, roast pig, applesauce, pies, and puddings were some of the foods served at the bees.

9. Pioneers usually baked bread from wheat flour, but sometimes they used corn, rye, or buckwheat.

10. Some people in the 1830s thought rubbing a potato on a wart would make the wart go away.

My little cousin says that rubbing a penny on a wart gets rid of it. –E.

So You Want to Know...

FROM AUTHOR FRIEDA WISHINSKY

When I was writing this book, my friends wanted to know more about pioneer travel and life in Upper Canada. I told them that all the characters in *Stop that Stagecoach!* were made up, but that the events were based on real settlers' journals, books, and experiences, including those of pioneer sisters Susanna Moodie and Catharine Parr Traill. Here are other questions I answered about what happened to new settlers on their journey to Canada.

Why did people immigrate to Canada from Britain in the 1830s?

Life in those days could be difficult for young people unless you had family money. Even in a wealthy family, if you were a younger son, you probably wouldn't inherit land or money. Then in the early 1800s, "Canadian mania" swept through Britain, which at that time included Ireland along with England, Wales, and Scotland. People raved about the beauty of the country and were excited to hear about the free land offered to young men who'd returned home after the Napoleonic Wars. Many leaped at the chance to try their luck. So off they sailed to Canada, either alone or with their family.

What was the trip like to Upper Canada?

It was a lot like the journey described in *Stop that Stagecoach!* The voyage across the Atlantic was miserable and crowded. There was little fresh food or water. Some people became ill and some died aboard ship. Once the settlers arrived in Canada, they were often packed into rickety stagecoaches and jostled while travelling on the rutted and bumpy Upper Canada roads. These "corduroy" roads were made of round logs, placed side by side over muddy or rough sections. Carriages sank in the mud and got stuck in the gaps between the logs. The inns along the roads were generally dirty, and offered little privacy. The trip from Montreal took weeks. Today it would take only hours.

What was Upper Canada like in the 1830s?

It was vast and sparsely populated by settlers. There were few towns, and most, like Brockville and Kingston, were near the shores of the St. Lawrence. These small towns consisted of a few mills, a couple of stores, a small church, a smithy (a blacksmith's workshop), and sometimes a local newspaper. Most people's houses were wooden shanties with only a few rooms.

Did life get easier once settlers arrived in their new homes?

Life was never easy for settlers. It was hard for many newcomers to adapt to the rough living conditions in the wilderness and the harsh, long winters in Canada. Women often gave birth to many children. Everyone in the family worked hard on the farms, and yet most settlers still had money worries. But even though life was tough, and neighbours didn't always live close by, people would help each other build a new house or barn, or take care of a sick relative.

What was it like to prepare food in Upper Canada?

People had to cook over an open flame in a fireplace. Kettles and pots hung by hooks over the fire, but flat-bottomed pans were placed right on the flame. Meat was suspended on a string over the fire. You had to be careful cooking this way. You could easily get singed, scalded, or burned. Fresh vegetables were only available for part of the year, but people stored root vegetables (like potatoes, carrots, and turnips) in a root cellar or in a pit in the ground. Meat and fruit like apples were dried so they could be eaten all year round.

Why were "bees" such an important part of settler life?

Bees were big, noisy working parties. Neighbours gathered to assist each other in building a house or barn. Joining together to do back-breaking tasks like chopping wood or to do tedious chores like husking corn made the work easier. Women enjoyed the socializing at quilting or sewing bees. They shared remedies for illnesses, advice about children, and gossip.

Coming next in the
Canadian Flyer Adventures Series...

Canadian Flyer Adventures #14

SOS! Titanic!

Can Matt and Emily save the Titanic from colliding with an iceberg?

For a sneak peek at the latest book in the series, visit:
www.owlkids.com
and click on the red maple leaf!

The *Canadian Flyer Adventures* Series

#1 Beware, Pirates!

#2 Danger, Dinosaurs!

#3 Crazy for Gold

#4 Yikes, Vikings!

#5 Flying High!

#6 Pioneer Kids

#7 Hurry, Freedom

#8 A Whale Tale

#9 All Aboard!

#10 Lost in the Snow

#11 Far from Home

#12 On the Case

#13 Stop that Stagecoach!

Upcoming Book

Look out for the next book that will take Emily and Matt on a new adventure:

#14 SOS! Titanic!

And more to come!

More Praise for the Series

"[Emily and Matt] learn more than they ever could have from a history textbook. Every book in this new series promises to shed light on a different chapter of Canadian history."
~ *MONTREAL GAZETTE*

"Readers are in for a great adventure."
~ *EDMONTON'S CHILD*

"This series makes Canadian history fun, exciting and accessible."
~ *CHRONICLE HERALD (HALIFAX)*

"[An] enthralling series for junior-school readers."
~ *HAMILTON SPECTATOR*

"...highly entertaining, very educational but not too challenging. A terrific new series."
~ *RESOURCE LINKS*

"This wonderful new Canadian historical adventure series combines magic and history to whisk young readers away on adventure...A fun way to learn about Canada's past."
~ *BC PARENT*

"Highly recommended."
~ *CM: CANADIAN REVIEW OF MATERIALS*

Teacher Resource Guides now available online. Please visit our website at **www.owlkids.com** and click on the red maple leaf to download tips and ideas for using the series in the classroom.

About the Author

Frieda Wishinsky, a former teacher, is an award-winning picture- and chapter-book author, who has written many beloved and bestselling books for children. Frieda enjoys using humour and history in her work, while exploring new ways to tell a story. Her books have earned much critical praise, including a nomination for a Governor General's Award in 1999. In addition to the books in the *Canadian Flyer Adventures* series, Frieda has published *What's the Matter with Albert?*, *A Quest in Time*, and *Manya's Dream* with Maple Tree Press. Frieda lives in Toronto.

About the Illustrator

Jean-Paul Eid has been drawing for as long as he can remember. From a very young age he dreamed of becoming a comic book artist, and liked to doodle cartoon characters of his teachers in the margins of his school workbooks. At the age of 20, he published his first comic in a magazine. Since then, he has published four award-winning graphic novels as well as several books for children. He has also done illustrations for museums, children's magazines, and film productions. Jean-Paul lives in Montreal, Quebec, with his two children, Mathilde and Axel.